ASH ISLAND

WALLACE & FRANTZ

SURSUM CORDA PRESS

Artwork licensed to Sursum Corda Press by Abigail K. See

Cover design by Cassidy Wierks

To everyone who
has experienced the heartache of
shipwrecks in this life,

May the Lord our God be your victorious warrior
and Abba Father...

"We have this hope as an anchor for the soul,
firm and secure."
Hebrews 6:19

WALLACE & FRANTZ

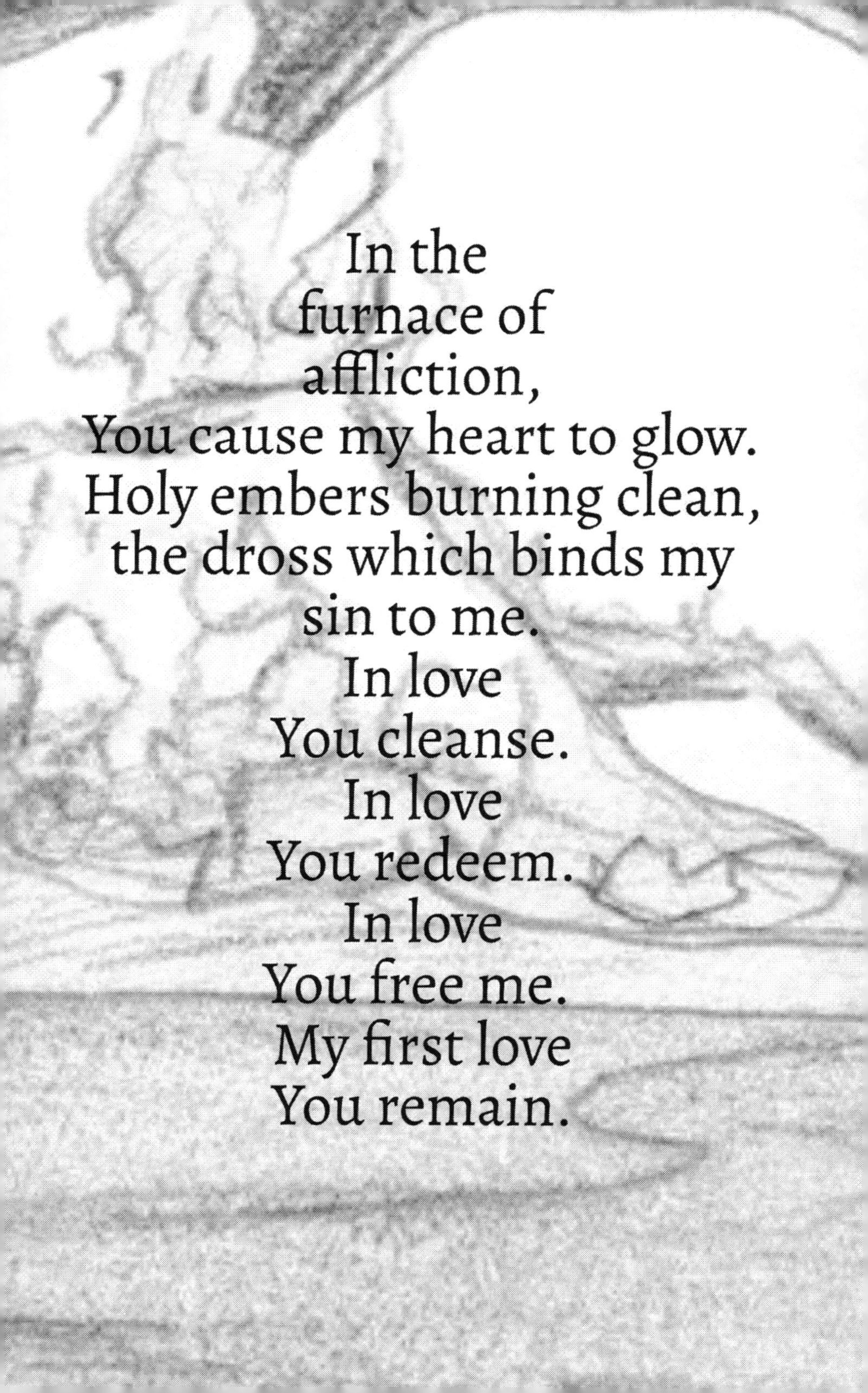

In the
furnace of
affliction,
You cause my heart to glow.
Holy embers burning clean,
the dross which binds my
sin to me.
In love
You cleanse.
In love
You redeem.
In love
You free me.
My first love
You remain.

I would go to the deeps a
hundred times to
cheer a downcast spirit.
It is good for me to have been
afflicted,
that I might know how to speak a word
in season to one that
is weary.

Charles Spurgeon

ASH ISLAND
The falls
Hill of rest
Crown of beauty
N
W
E
S

Chapter 1

SWEPT OVERBOARD

"The sea was getting rougher and rougher."
Jonah 1:11a

The storm emerged on the horizon, as if from nowhere. But wait, that wasn't wholly true. Its current-charged scent had raised the hairs on the back of her neck.

Even though the sun shone and warmed her, she shivered at the growing awareness of the storm's potential danger.

She nimbly climbed high into the lookout. There it was, an ever-increasing smudge blotting out the blue sky. Under her spotless linen cloak, she took out the spyglass she wore at her side, a gift from her King. Removing its leather sheathing and lens cover, she telescoped it open. Gulls raced landward before the growing storm.

Normally she could instantly calculate how far away the refracted image was, but not this time. She shut the spyglass with a hard slap and returned it to its home.

Perhaps it will pass by.

Her thoughts clouded with little hope.

Maybe that's why I can't tell how far away it is?

As the wind changed direction, the main sail snapped, flapping to attention always eager to obey. But a heavy foreboding blanketed her.

Why? She wondered.

Though this was her first solo mission, she'd encountered smaller storms and weathered them, why should this be any different? Her ship was powerful and well supplied. It surely wouldn't fail her.

She looked across the well-scrubbed deck. The freshly oiled wood was clean and glowing. Barrels of freshly stocked provisions lay stacked in two neat rows. Secure knots held them fast to the deck.

Her ship's banner waved in the growing breeze. Proudly, it rode atop the gleaming mast for every eye to behold — *Servant of the King.*

Silver threads emblazoned on blue silk spelled out the truth she knew to her core. And yet, she felt a growing uneasiness she couldn't quite fathom. She must find a safe cove, just like those seabirds racing for shelter.

From a leather pouch about her waist, she retrieved a map and unfolded it. This was another gift she'd received on the day of her new birth.

The King not only transformed her heart of stone to a living, beating, flesh-heart, but He equipped her with everything necessary for this voyage — a trusty ship, navigation tools, a trunk of new clothes, spyglass, some jewelry, her sword and scabbard, and perhaps the most treasured, her map.

And according to the latter, an island was nearby, Ash Island. She adjusted her sails and did something Christa Lea never did — she sped for shelter as the storm intensified.

Lightning cracked overhead as the sky simultaneously darkened. Churning clouds eclipsed the sun. Darker and darker it became until it was dark as night.

The warrior princess ran blind, her cape whipping in the wind. She twisted it thin and tucked it into her leather belt. Her heart thundered in her chest as the storm engulfed her.

The boat creaked and moaned in protest as the waves pushed violently toward the island. She lurched onto the foredeck and grasped the wheel. Sheets of rain blinded her further, soaking her from head to toe.

For one of the first times in her many voyages for her King, she felt a bone-paralyzing fear. She, who endured many hardships and vanquished serpents, had never faced this kind of unbridled fury before.

"I am too weak for this," she muttered under her breath.

Not that anyone would have heard above the din of the storm. She could scream at the heavens and no one would hear.

Still the storm raged. For hours, the wave-tossed ship rolled back and forth, knocking her down and bruising her many times. Just as she came to the end of her strength, an enormous wave washed over the side, knocking her from her rightful place.

Down she plummeted into the dark sea. The cape twisted tightly about her and stole her breath. The depths swallowed her spyglass, sword, and map.

Her last conscious thoughts braided into an echoing refrain of how could this be and why — this dark rope intertwined and took her under.

My Anchor Holds

"Servant of the King" was emblazoned on the ship's banner. Yet it did not spare Christa Lea from this storm. In Mark 6 just after Jesus fed the 5,000, we read,

"Immediately Jesus made his disciples get into the boat and go on ahead of him to Bethsaida, while he dismissed the crowd. After leaving them, he went up on a mountainside to pray. Later that night, the boat was in the middle of the lake, and he was alone on land. He saw the disciples straining at the oars, because the wind was against them" (Mark 6:45-48).

The Lord left his servants, his much-loved disciples, to row against the wind for hours. The wise, loving Lord sent them out before dark and waited until "shortly before dawn" to go out to them. Don't miss this: the disciples were in this hard place not because they had been disobedient to their Master, but because they had obeyed his call to cross the lake.

"You hurled me into the depths,
into the very heart of the seas,
and the currents swirled about me;
all your waves and breakers
swept over me."
Jonah 2:3

Have you ever been surprised when the King sent you into a storm?

___

___

___

If we have been given new hearts, we are like Christa Lea, equipped "with everything necessary for this voyage." How does this truth make you feel?

___

___

___

___

___

When have you felt like Christa Lea: engulfed, either physically or spiritually, in wild, uncontrolled waves?

___

___

___

Chapter 2

Ash Island

"You will be secure, because there is hope; you will look about you and take your rest in safety."
Job 11:18

When Christa Lea awoke she was on land — laying belly down and slightly askew. Salt stung her eyes and lips. Her right hand lay inert on the black sand. She choked up brackish water, took a deep breath, and hacked up more.

Relief swept over her to see the golden ring given to her the day of the ship-launch.

Over the last eight years, she'd worn it on her middle finger and had never removed it — the anchor imprinted on its golden face reminded her of His promises.

She remembered her boat launch ceremony as if it was yesterday — her heart swelled with love and gratitude as she gazed into the King's eyes. The ship and gifts secondary in her affections. She'd rested her face against His broad chest as His powerful arms enfolded her. Now, her face rest against burnt ash making an unlikely pillow. Had she done something wrong? Something to displease Him?

She drew in a mouthful of seawater lapping against her shoulder, swished it about, and spit it out. Her shredded tunic was the only remaining covering. Odd bits of shell and seaweed adorned one arm like a lady's glove. She rolled over and gazed into the sky, groaning in pain. Her whole body ached like one enormous bruise.

Overhead, the sky was an overcast slate ceiling. An eerie silence pervaded the charred air. It was incredibly still. She flicked the bits off her hand, only to find smudges of ash remained.

"Well, I suppose it isn't called Ash Island for nothing," she mused aloud.

The more she rubbed, the more stained her skin became. Wherever she touched her arm... nose... forehead... became a forest of smudges. She groaned again, this time in frustration.

Whatever.

Christa Lea shifted gingerly and sat up, checking for broken bones — none jutted out or lay askew. There were a few cuts including one worrisome deep tear in her calf. She quickly tore a linen strip from her sleeve, wrung the water from her hair as best she could, and tied her long auburn hair into a low side ponytail out of the way.

Her frank blue eyes moved back to the deep gash. She winced as she touched its inflamed edges. Blood wept from the wound. Tearing another wider strip of linen, she bound it staunching its flow.

She stood up shakily. Her head ached — a wave of dizziness and nausea passed. Christa Lea slowly surveyed the land, remembering from her map its relative size. Just a small sliver amid an expansive sea.

How will they find me? She stared across the empty, lonely horizon.

These were unchartered-to-her waters. And her tools were lost! How would she navigate the island without a map? How was she to serve her King here?

She peered up and down the shoreline. Everything was ashy terrain, with odd bits of flotsam marring the ebony landscape. Steep, rocky cliffs lined the shore. A lone, active volcano graced the north end of the island, puffing steady wisps of smoke. A twin sat silent beside it. She knew the island to be uninhabited and forsaken.

Forsaken — that would be a more accurate name. This was not a typical place to land.

She hugged her elbows to her chest, smudging them even more.

Ash. She sighed deeply.

It's rightly named, but... but I am forsaken.

As Christa Lea absorbed this truth, a single tear became a torrent. She wept for a long time.

My Anchor Holds

This chapter opens with Christa Lea recovering her ring—a ring imprinted with an anchor. The anchor represents hope. Hebrews 6:19a assures "We have this hope as an anchor for the soul, firm and secure."

How is hope in Jesus Christ like an anchor for your soul?

____

____

____

____

____

____

____

"Though my father and mother forsake me, the LORD will receive me." Psalm 27:10

Forsaken. It means to be abandoned forever. Has a friend or family member forsaken you?

Friends and family may forsake us. But the great truth, the truth that Christa Lea doesn't see, is that the LORD will never forsake his own. How can we gird up our minds so that sad feelings, even feelings of forsakenness, don't block out the truth of God's presence?

Chapter 3

THIRST

"I am poured out like water, and all my bones are out of joint. My heart has turned to wax; it has melted within me."
Psalm 22:14

After her inner storm subsided, Christa Lea wiped her eyes, smudging her appearance even more. Her tattered linen shift was streaked with the stuff.

Whatever, she thought. *I smell and look like the old charwoman who cleans the King's hearth.*

She stumbled along the beach, her toes and feet gritty and grimy, caked in ash. Her throat burned with thirst.

She looked to the right and left. Black ash sand extended in both directions. The only difference were the volcanoes to her left, marking the north end of the island. Muttering a small prayer, she waited a moment, then headed south.

A heavy disorientation made it difficult to focus, but even though her head swam, she pressed forward. Ahead, a rivulet opened into the sea. The small stream meandered down between black dunes, yielding to grey volcanic rock further up and back. She stumbled forward and climbed carefully, yet eagerly. Her feet, knees, and hands were further covered in ash.

As she climbed up the stepping sheets of rock, she found its origin. A spring-fed pool welcomed her into a quiet hollow. She cupped her hands and drank a small mouthful, testing to see if it was potable or poison.

Oh — sweet relief. The water tasted clean. She sipped several handfuls, then laid back on a stone slab, overcome by exhaustion. Coming this far had taken everything out of her.

Blood loss. Dehydration. Having been trained in the healing arts, she knew the signs well. She rolled onto her side and drank another handful.

Christa Lea dozed off and dreamt of the storm. In a feverish delirium, she relived its terror over and over. She tried to outrun the storm, to no avail. Her cape wrapped around her neck, choking the life from her. She vainly wrestled seaweed. It wrapped around her and dragged her down into the watery depths as a suffocating pressure tossed and turned her. Her map grew to the size of a whale and swallowed her. Her spyglass wouldn't work, time after time.

In the great depths of darkness, each gift betrayed and devoured her. Hours turned to days in semi-conscious stupor. She finally awoke.

Time was indistinguishable, the sun hidden behind a perpetual dull grayness. Morning... afternoon... evening... she had no way of knowing. Had time stopped? Was she trapped in an unending moment of grief? She drank again from the pool and despite her questions, His peace filled her.

After removing what little clothing remained, along with the bandage, she waded into its shallow depths and lay down. Blood wept from her wound in gentle, pulsing rivulets. A battle hymn she'd sung many times surfaced. "Oh, precious is the flow that makes me white as snow..."

She rubbed her hands together in the water, but the ash didn't budge.

She climbed out and rinsed the bandage, tightly wrapping it around the wound. It was healing. She cleaned her garment and laid it on the rock to dry. Self-conscious of her nakedness, she looked around. But there was no one. No lizards, no birds, nothing. Just her. Had the seabirds found shelter?

Christa Lea closed her eyes and slept again. She dreamt once more of the storm. The weight of the dark depths pressing and crushing her small form as it relentlessly choked and rolled her within the underwater prison. Its deep darkness engulfing and tossing her like flotsam. She woke with a start, heart pounding. She slowly inhaled.

This wasn't the assignment written in my scroll.

After all, it had mentioned a fellow warrior. Had there been a mistake? Doubt colored her thoughts.

A rumble in her stomach interrupted the useless flow of questions. She tried chewing a rope of seaweed. It proved tough and rubbery, inedible. Her shift was dry. She pulled it over her head and tied the seaweed around her waist. Rising, she returned the short distance to the beach and, noting where the spring lay, headed south.

My Anchor Holds

Sweet relief. We may have to wait to experience God's presence or comfort. Yet here Christa Lea is restored by crucial life-giving springs, by refreshment in the ashes. "I will refresh the weary and satisfy the faint" (Jeremiah 31:25). Have you experienced this? When?

After she drank, Christa Lea slept. In her nightmare, "each gift betrayed and devoured her." Without knowing how the story unfolds, how might this foreshadow or cast spiritual light on her life?

"For he has not despised or scorned
the suffering of the afflicted one;
he has not hidden his face from him
but has listened to his cry for help."
Psalm 22:24

Portions of Psalm 22 were quoted by Jesus as he hung, forsaken by the Father, on the cross. Yet this verse is different. How do these words encourage you?

CHAPTER 4
HUNGER

"THE WAVES OF DEATH SWIRLED ABOUT ME; THE TORRENTS OF DESTRUCTION OVERWHELMED ME."
2 SAMUEL 22:5

Large, craggy rocks lay before her — a forest of obsidian spires twisted upward to sharp peaks. Christa Lea walked along the water's edge where the ash sand was more gentle on bare feet. Much easier than trying to climb through the impassable spiky maze.

The beach abruptly ended in solid rock halting her progress. She hesitated a moment, then entered the calm water and swam along the rock wall.

Swish, swish, the water gently lapped against it. As she rounded the promontory, she spied another ash beach.

A large cape opened before her. Outlined by high cliffs, its cove was deep. And there was her boat — or rather, what remained.

She climbed out of the water and faltered onto the beach, her heart in her throat. Her beloved ship lay wrecked in the rocky bay, cracked open like a large geode.

"My ship! My beautiful ship!"

Overwhelmed, she fell to her knees.

A single tear traced its way down the contours of her face. She wiped it aside as anger welled within her. She considered the sails. They hung as listless scraps... worthless. Loud creaks and moans drifted on the breeze, the boat echoing her own protests.

The figurehead on its bow, carved by skilled artisans, sat akimbo, astride a reef. It lay at an unnatural angle, broken and splintered.

"Why, my King? What have I done to deserve this?" she sighed.

No answer came, no comforting breeze stirred. Silence reigned, its stillness all-engulfing as Christa Lea considered the loss. Her stomach tightened as she wrestled with the unchangeable truth before her in the bay.

Whatever then.

If the boat was closer she would swim out and check for provisions. Instead, she scanned the beach. Something lay ahead, bobbing in the water near the shore. She was growing weak again from the exertion of the swim and trek, but hunger propelled her as she stood then stumbled forward.

When she reached it, she found it was one of her barrels of provisions. She pushed it ashore, pried the lid off, and was relieved to find an unharmed cask of dried fish.

Christa Lea mumbled a half-hearted prayer and ate until she was full. Her hunger assuaged, she washed her hands in the nearby water and shook them dry. She lay down and fell unconscious again.

Hours later she awoke.

Had anything else washed ashore?

As she walked along, her toe caught on something. She tripped and fell. The pain startled a curse from her lips as fresh blood wept into the lone bandage on her calf.

What...

As Christa Lea pulled the loop out of the sand, she saw it was part of the blue silk banner — Servant of the King.

Then why this... this wreckage and pain?

A flood of questions breached the surface.

"Haven't I faithfully served You?" she railed heavenward as tears welled and overflowed.

She only wanted to hear His praise: "Well done, oh, good and faithful servant."

Was this so wrong?

Others had been rewarded with wreaths upon their heads — Crowns of Joy. But here she was a wounded wreck.

Tears streamed down her cheeks, leaving clean trails amid the ash smudges. She'd always despised tears, considering them a sign of weakness. After all, she was the child of a Warrior Lord and his Lady — no weakling. Wiping her eyes, Christa Lea was startled to see her hands washed clean by the tears.

"It figures," she said in resignation.

My Anchor Holds

"What have I done to deserve this?" Christa Lea wondered. When life crashes into us, we wonder too. Do you think this is a helpful question for us to ask? Why or why not?

Part of the ship's banner, the part reading, "Servant of the King" was buried in ashy sand. How is this symbolic?

"Well done, good and faithful servant." Matthew 25:21a

Can you relate to Christa Lea who only wanted to hear her King say, "Well done, good and faithful servant" (Matthew 25:21a)?

CHAPTER 5

BROKENNESS

"THEREFORE I WILL NOT KEEP SILENT; I WILL SPEAK OUT IN THE ANGUISH OF MY SPIRIT, I WILL COMPLAIN IN THE BITTERNESS OF MY SOUL."
JOB 7:11

Although the days, weeks, and months sped on, she felt stuck. This unsought pause caused her to question the King's character.

Why would He allow this?

For generations, her ancestors had courageously served Him. Her parents were great and mighty warriors. Others, esteemed teachers and judges.

When she'd come of age, this legacy passed to her. A desire to serve Him had allied with a growing awareness that as King, it was His due.

She'd grown up aboard her parent's mighty ship. High on the mast, the crimson silk banner threaded with gold embroidery declared the vessel's name — *Victorious*. A noble heritage.

Her face burned as thoughts assailed and judged her, relentless as the storm. What would her family think if they saw her in this place of naked weakness trapped on this forsaken island of burnt shame?

Her steady stream of tears cleansed her skin, only to be soiled again by the ash coating everything.

I'm just a charred stick discarded on this ash heap.

Christa Lea scanned the surroundings. The burnt odor permeated everything — and was inescapable.

"It smells of despair," she whispered.

The moments blurred together in a jumble — sleeping, crying, eating, crying, swimming to the spring to drink and to bathe. A creature of habit, she found comfort in completing tasks.

Whatever.

Even as her wound healed, leaving her with a slight limp, a thorn of bitterness lodged deep within her heart. So deep she wasn't aware of it, and if she had known she wouldn't have cared anyway.

As the days flipped past, unbidden tears grew familiar. Deep grief and weariness settled over her shoulders like a heavy cloak.

She quit fighting the tears. Instead, she welcomed them. In her weakness, her heart softened. Soft enough that a hard shaft of something lodged deep was becoming discernible to Christa Lea.

This was a new lesson. She'd heard whispers of inglorious assignments where compassion deepened but she never desired them. Now, she tasted it and found it filling and warm with a slight tang, like her mother's sourdough bread fresh from the oven.

The tang came from the regret that surfaced as she considered past thoughts and actions.

How many hollow words of comfort have I spoken and how many error-filled judgments have I made?

These realizations gave her the greatest pangs of all. In the humbling, she deepened. And the deeper she went, the more humbled she became.

"What shallow waters I've been swimming in," she confessed out loud.

Tattered coverings hung on her ash-smudged, gaunt frame.

"No one would recognize me now, not even my brothers and sisters," she said while examining her hands.

Ash covered palms...

Torn fingernails...

Christa Lea twisted the anchor ring easily about her middle finger. Her saltwater bleached hair, coated in grimy ash, hung knotted past her shoulders.

What a freak I must look!

And she did.

She sat down and slipped the ring off easily. She rolled it along the lip of the scar on her calf. Its raised edge delineated her past life from this present reality. She slipped it back on.

This solitary life with its unending quiet wasn't comfortable. Christa Lea missed the celebration banquets that used to mark successful work.

Do they miss me? Are they even praying?

Her memories evaporated like mist before the sun.

She considered the ring. It was a very tangible reminder with its inscribed anchor mooring her to the past's truth. But out in the bay lay the broken ship's useless remains.

The chattering questions continued incessantly, harassing and making her doubt the truth. She reminded herself it hadn't been that long ago.

Food-laced daydreams of roast beef and potatoes, bread with fresh creamed butter, plus crispy greens with oil and vinegar taunted her. She'd read in the King's Book about the wandering of the Israelites and His provision of manna in the wilderness. Now she understood their complaints. Oh, how she understood.

Fish and water, the very meal her Savior had served so many while on earth was becoming a detested thing. Like the Brussels sprouts her mother made her eat in childhood.

Her mother's voice echoed in her memories, "Be grateful. There are others who aren't so fortunate. They would give anything for even one." Her pouty frown answered. But now, she would give anything for one of her mom's buttery, seasoned sprouts.

As the days passed Christa Lea searched the horizon, but still no one came. Memories kept washing ashore, but not much else. Just some brown leather and an undyed tunic.

With a rock she'd scraped the leather thin and supple and fashioned low boots, a bag for fish, and a satchel for water. With sharpened pieces of obsidian, she'd pierced holes for laces and planned to cut long, thin strips to use as thread for sewing the seams. These projects were almost complete.

With the food supply diminishing, she would need to explore the east side of the island. She would keep the rescued tunic for that day.

My Anchor Holds

Suffering and pain can easily morph into self-pity and bitterness. What is the difference between pouring out our hearts to God, which Psalm 62:8 invites us to do, and self-focused sulking?

____

____

____

____

In the book of Lamentations, written during the exile of God's people, we read, "'My splendor is gone and all that I had hoped from the LORD.' I remember my affliction and my wandering, the bitterness and the gall. I well remember them, and my soul is downcast within me" (Lamentations 3:18-20). What place does lament have in your life?

____

____

____

"Trust in him at all times, you people;
pour out your hearts to him,
for God is our refuge."
Psalm 62:8

Left alone to reflect, Christa Lea began to see herself, and her words of comfort and judgment in a new, humbling light. Is there a difference between being humbled and being humble? Or, when we are humbled as Christa Lea was, is it inevitable that we will become humble?

Chapter 6

Leaving the Cove

"Blessed are those who mourn,
for they will be comforted."
Matthew 5:4

Three sleepings ago Christa Lea finished the leather pieces. Slipping on the makeshift leather boots, she admired her handiwork.

Though they were nowhere near as fine as what she used to own, they offered protection from jagged rocks and would be helpful for climbing.

Clothing herself in the fresh tunic, she tied a strip of the old one around her waist as a belt. She filled her water-skin then plugged it with seaweed.

The satchel contained the last of the dried fish — 12 pieces. She tied it closed and placed both over her shoulders cross body style. She tied her hair back in a low ponytail with a piece of the remaining silk from her once beautiful banner.

With limited food, she knew it was time. She walked to the east end of the cove as far as she could. It was the farthest she'd been. Looking back at her temporary home and her broken ship one last time, a solitary tear slid down her cheek as she whispered, "Goodbye..."

She placed the anchor ring on her thumb for security — fearful of losing another gift — and turning back toward the steep, obsidian cliffs, she waded into the water and swam along its edge.

Careful to keep an arm's length away from the wall of sharp rock, she fell into a steady rhythm as the quiet waves set a gentle tempo. Swimming between sleep cycles had succeeded in strengthening the muscles in her weak leg.

She'd succeeded. After all, physical conditioning was nothing new to her. She'd trained hard since her youth.

Under her parent's tutelage, she learned a warrioress must remain in peak condition to serve the King well. All her life she accompanied them on assignments with her siblings. This combination had prepared her well for the present hardships.

She kept up a steady pace for what seemed an age. Rounding the long cliff, she stopped and tread in place. Before her lay an oasis. Lush, green overgrowth filled this hilly side of the island.

Tears streamed from her eyes.

Praise the King!

As she drew nearer, she could see palm trees and sea grass dotting the beach. Excited, she swam faster.

But up ahead was something she hadn't expected. She squinted in disbelief.

There, further up the beach, a man squat next to the fire. He stood and beckoned her with the wave of his arm.

As she came out of the water, she adjusted her shift and her bags, self-conscious of her scant covering.

Whatever, it couldn't be helped.

Wringing the water from her hair, she walked toward him. This beach was only sprinklings of ash mixed in with fresh sand. Its washed pebbles and shards of shell were a welcome change.

As she drew nearer, she noted he was clean. His silver-flecked beard and loosely braided brown hair were both long and free of ash.

He raised his right arm and pointed heavenward with his first two fingers crossed, then placed them over his heart. She returned the salute — a familiar greeting between subjects of the King. She was never so happy to see another person.

A warm glow filled her chest for the first time since the storm. Oh, how good it felt. He smiled back. His weathered face was one of the most handsome she'd ever seen.

My Anchor Holds

Desperation drives us on. But always God leads. When have you been forced to move from a familiar place or people and found Psalm 23 to be true? That "surely goodness and mercy" were following you?

Sometimes we don't see the value in our discipline, our training, in the moment. Hebrews 12:10b-11 says, "God disciplines us for our good, in order that we may share in his holiness. No discipline seems pleasant at the time, but painful. Later on, however, it produces a harvest of righteousness and peace for those who have been trained by it."

"Surely your goodness and love will follow me all the days of my life, and I will dwell in the house of the Lord forever."
Psalm 23:6

Christa Lea's physical training proved helpful as she swam. In what challenging situation can you trust that your current training will prove productive later?

Have you ever experienced the joy of a meeting with a fellow son or daughter of the King when you least expected it?

Chapter 7

Meeting William

"A young man, wearing nothing but
a linen garment, was following Jesus."
Mark 14:51

He was taller by a good head or so and at least 10 years older. Lean and tan, he wore a simple grey linen cloak. Under this was a similar rough, homespun cotton tunic and pants.

As she approached, he removed his cloak and as she drew near he averted his gaze and covered her. Embarrassed by her lack of clothing, she welcomed it.

"Hullo and welcome. I am William, Keeper of Ash Island."

Next to the fire a coarse blanket was spread out. A loaf of bread sat on a wooden platter with a jug of wine and two carved cups. He motioned for her to sit.

"I'm Christa Lea." She inhaled the earthy scent of freshly baked bread. It smelled wonderful.

Raising the loaf heavenward, he broke it and gave thanks. Half he handed to her. A deep peace warmed her as she ate.

Filling both cups with wine, he gave thanks again, "As often as we drink this, our Lord and Savior, we do so in remembrance of You."

She bowed her head and drank the wine. Its warmth spread through her, reminding her of their King's many mercies.

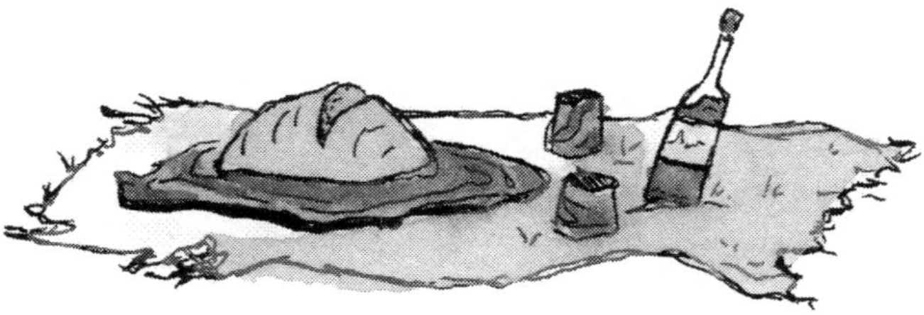

As they ate before the fire, she shared the story of her shipwreck on Ash Island. She was more hungry for fellowship than she'd realized. He listened and thoughtfully questioned Christa Lea, drawing her story out.

When she finished telling the history of the storm, and how she'd spent her days since, it was his turn to explain his presence.

"I am William, current solitary of Ash Island and Guardian of the Pass. I've been stationed here many a year by the King's decree and I've enjoyed the privilege of serving those whom He sends."

Christa Lea had heard of hermits at outposts. She'd always thought it a wasteful assignment — living in seclusion. How much more could they have accomplished in a heavily populated area?

Embarrassed at the thought, she blushed. His presence was so welcome. She hoped she'd never again judge so quickly.

Suddenly at her internal admission, sunlight pierced the clouds illuminating a small hill close to the north end. Just past it one of the volcanoes smoldered and rumbled.

William looked at her knowingly. Her confession resulted in the shaft of light, and he knew it. He pointed to the hill.

"That's where my home is."

A thought occurred to Christa Lea. "Did you expect me? This fire? The bread and drink? It's like you were waiting."

"Yes," he said plainly, "I was expecting you. I have been for quite some time. But my sentinel is to wait here and come no farther south."

She hesitated before asking, "Just how long have you been waiting?"

"I've been aware of your presence since the storm blew you in. I saw your ship racing in front of it and then I witnessed the storm engulf it. When there are survivors, they always wash up on Ash Beach. It has been six months and four days," he said, watching her reaction.

"He told me your time to cross would come, and you would need me. So I began my preparations for your visit. This has afforded me ample time. His ways are always so."

My Anchor Holds

"His ways are always so."

You prepare a table before me. "I go to prepare a place for you," Jesus told his disciples. It requires faith to believe these truths when we reside on Ash Beach, but they are all true. Do you believe that a good table awaits on the other side of the island?

"He guides the humble in what is right and teaches them his way."
Psalm 25:9

Psalm 112:4 says, "Even in darkness light dawns for the upright." When did the light pierce the clouds in this chapter?

In Scripture how are weakness and humility related to God's guidance and light?

CHAPTER 8

INNER WORKINGS

"BECAUSE YOU ARE HIS SONS, GOD SENT THE SPIRIT OF HIS SON INTO OUR HEARTS, THE SPIRIT WHO CALLS OUT, 'ABBA, FATHER.'"
GALATIANS 4:6

Shivereing, she wrapped his woolen cloak tightly about her. It was hard to accept she'd been on the island such a long time.

"All my friends must think me dead," she whispered.

"Perhaps," he said with his chin set firmly, "but that is more than I know. Come, if you feel strong enough, let's go home."

She nodded and lifted the bread board. Crumbs fell to the sand. They rinsed the wooden goblets in the gently lapping waves, shook them dry, and laid the meal items in the center of the blanket. He rolled it up expertly.

A leather strap buckled the package securely. He fed a piece of rope through it and tied it in a closed loop. This he slung over his arms like a backpack.

Christa Lea admired his ingenuity as she watched the travel rite carried out with such fluid movements. She had never conceived that such a mundane task could be so artistically performed.

Or was it just the beauty of another living, breathing soul? She corrected herself. *No, there was more.*

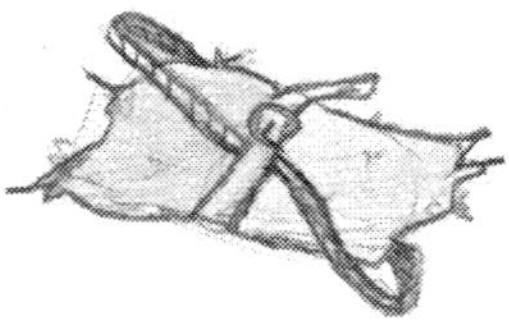

As she watched further she realized all his actions were deliberate and thoughtful. Little pebbles of prayer fell from his lips as he went about his tasks. She could see his love for their King was genuine. A rare smile lit her face.

His prayers were constant and peace-filled, yet every once in a while Christa Lea heard an unfamiliar word surface.

"What does that word mean?"

"Which?" he asked.

"Abba?" she wondered, the word felt soft on her lips.

He stopped what he was doing and faced her.

"Do you not know?" he asked with concern.

"I think I've heard it before, but I'm not sure..." she truthfully confessed.

He answered, "It means "daddy" or "father" — the most precious name for our King."

Anger flared inside her and she burst out, "What father allows his daughter to lose all her gifts and wash ashore on this forsaken island?"

A numb weight settled over her chest even as her cheeks flushed with deep shame. The bitter torrent had carried her away just as the storm had. Her arms dropped heavily to her sides.

He turned and slowly picked up his walking staff — his lips moving in silent prayer. Her reaction, though common for those stranded here, stretched his patience.

She is His child too, he reminded himself, *you would do well to remember that.*

He looked back at her with such sorrow that part of her anger subsided. Without a word, he nodded and motioned for her to come.

She finished gathering her items and placed the bags over the borrowed cloak she wore. Considering her limited options, she followed.

My Anchor Holds

When we become God's children, He places his Spirit in our hearts. It is his "seal of ownership on us, and put his Spirit in our hearts as a deposit, guaranteeing what is to come" (2 Corinthians 1:22). Why do we need this guarantee of our future inheritance?

"The Spirit you received does not make you slaves, so that you live in fear again; rather, the Spirit you received brought about your adoption to sonship. And by him we cry, 'Abba, Father.'"
Romans 8:15

"What father allows his daughter to lose all her gifts and wash ashore on this forsaken island?" Christa Lea asks what so many of us wonder. How would you answer yourself when this question surfaces?

"Abba" is a term of familial intimacy. It is a most intimate term for God. Jesus, God's only beloved Son, used it to address his Father the night he was betrayed in Gethsemane (Mark 14:36). How do you most often address God in prayer? Do you ever address God as Father?

CHAPTER 9

HEADING NORTH

"INSTEAD, SPEAKING THE TRUTH IN LOVE, WE WILL GROW TO BECOME... THE MATURE BODY OF HIM WHO IS THE HEAD, THAT IS, CHRIST."
EPHESIANS 4:15

The refining work of Ash Island always accomplished its purpose. William knew that. Why would it be any different with Christa Lea?

He'd felt such a tender kinship with her from the moment he looked into the pained hopefulness in her eyes. He felt it as she openly spoke about her struggles and disappointments. Her bitterness apparent even then. Though buried deep, it had to go.

He sighed. In renewed determination for her freedom and growth, he silently petitioned Abba for direction and wisdom.

Their King never failed, but nudges from the Holy Spirit warned this assignment was going to be different, and perhaps require something more from him.

A gentle breeze tousled his hair as they walked in silence along the beach. It comforted his questioning heart.

The overcast sky reigned over the island even after the first promising shaft illuminated his outpost near Steady Hill. The atmosphere heavy with foreboding.

Christa Lea looked at William. She was stuck with him, yet his presence didn't comfort her like she thought it should.

A few hours passed in this way. Silent, heavy, and awkward. They stopped and drank from her water-skin many times. After the last, she replaced the plug of seaweed and he broke the silence.

"We will go this way."

His finger pointed to a visible fork in the path leading toward the dense, green overgrowth. She nodded.

"Will we arrive at your home tonight?"

"No... well... it depends. Normally the stars are so beautiful from there..." He stopped, realizing they wouldn't see the stars until the clouds passed.

"You mean it's not always like this here? This heavy gray silence?" He shook his head and looked directly into her troubled blue eyes. They were stormy still — filled with fight.

"It came with you," he said, "and it will stay until you learn what you need to. That is the way of it here."

She cleared her throat, considered what he was implying, and spit out, "It's my fault?"

"That's not a helpful way to think about it. It's not about blame, but about growth... and surrender," he patiently answered.

Her ire, which had subsided, flashed again, *He equates these doldrums with me.*

"Would you hear me?" he asked. She tilted her head and took a protective stance. "Were not your words, out of your own mouth, that our Father took all your gifts away and brought you to a forsaken island?"

Well, yes. Wasn't it true? She nodded as he went to the heart of the matter.

"As a child of the King, should you make a habit of lying?"

This was just too much. She turned away fighting tears.

He gently grasped her arm and spoke quietly, "Did He take all your gifts?"

Turning her, he lifted her right hand. On it sat her ring. A fresh torrent of tears streamed from her eyes.

Have I wrongfully accused my King?

Shame washed over her for the second time today.

He pressed further, "Is this island forsaken?"

He released her hand and touched his chest.

"Has He not had His eye on you this entire time? Have we not been waiting for you?"

Racking sobs convulsed her as she considered the depth of her grievous sin.

And yet, she justified, "But my ship? My map? All my other gifts? They were mine!"

He listened to the silence before asking a surprising question, "What was the last thing you said to Him before this voyage?"

She wrinkled her brow, thinking.

In her memory, she approached the throne and knelt before the King. As His hand extended toward her, she kissed it.

"I will go anywhere for You, do anything, to show my love!" she promised.

He looked with kindness into her eyes and seeing into her heart, had asked, "Anywhere? Anything?"

"Yes," she'd asserted, "I am Your servant — ready for battle!"

Collapsing onto a nearby rock, the wind fell from her sails. How had she forgotten that conversation? When had her love for His gifts grown greater than her love for the King himself?

Was He exposing an underlying motive she'd never discerned? The possibility weakened her.

She bent forward onto her knees as tears left clean paths down her cheeks.

"Abba, forgive me..."

Her confession and repentance rose before His throne. Mercy prevailed. The thorn of bitterness embedded in her heart dissolved.

Shafts of light broke through the clouds as blue sky emerged. The sun had always been there. *He* had always been there. Peace flooded over her from head to toe.

William smiled and laid his hand on top of her head then uttered a heartfelt prayer, "We thank you, Father, for her repentance, and Your acceptance. You are our great treasure. Our salvation. Thank You."

She stood as a newfound lightness engulfed her — the unseen burden lifted. The King had never quit loving her. He had taken her at her word.

His Spirit whispered, "I discipline those whom I love — always in love. Didn't you desire to love Me more than all?"

She responded, knowing it was true ever since He breathed new life into her, "I do love You, Lord... My Treasure."

It had been so easy to promise in the beautiful palace, before His throne, gazing into His flaming wise eyes.

It was quite another thing when she was hurting and alone and obedience cost everything.

"I can't even love You without Your help," she confessed.

My Anchor Holds

So often we base our assessment of God's love on our feelings. We assume His love when we feel the sunshine. What truth did William share with Christa Lea about the persistent dark clouds?

Hebrews 12:6 says, the Lord disciplines the one he loves. Then the writer of Hebrews takes it a step further, adding that if we are not disciplined we are "not legitimate, not sure sons and daughters at all"(Hebrews 12:8). William urged Christa Lea, "to submit to the Father of spirits and live." How might a shift in our perspective on God's discipline enable us to receive God's will as "good, pleasing and perfect" (Romans 12:2)?

"Ye fearful saints fresh courage take,
the clouds that you much dread,
are big with mercy and shall break
in blessings on your head.

Judge not the Lord by feeble sense,
but trust him for his grace;
behind a frowning providence,
he hides a smiling face."

These words are from the hymn "God Moves in a Mysterious Way." It was written by William Cowper, a fellow saint who struggled to his death with depression. How could these images help you move through dark seasons?

Chapter 10

Heading Inland

"Therefore he is able to save completely those who come to God through him, because he always lives to intercede for them. Such a high priest truly meets our need — one who is holy, blameless, pure, set apart from sinners, exalted above the heavens."
Hebrews 7:25-26

"Come, Sister," he beckoned. "We still have far to go."

They continued along the path, weaving up and through grassy, palm-dotted dunes. As they approached the island's maritime forest, he pointed out varieties of trees and plants like a proud father showing off his child.

Night descended and they set up camp. William built a fire. After the breaking of bread and a dinner of fish, they gave thanks and slept.

Christa Lea fell into a deep, deep sleep. In her dream, she bowed before her gifts, desires, and glory. A dark shadow of shame crept over her as she realized they had become small gods.

The King appeared — with one hand He lifted her and with the other He swept her idols away.

"You are not the first to make this error, my child." He gazed into her eyes with tenderness.

She confessed her sin, weeping. "How can You still love me after I worshiped wrongly? How can You forgive me?"

In the dream, they stood at Golgotha, where His son died for her sins. An empty, blood-stained cross remained.

"It is finished. I save to the uttermost all who draw near to Me through Him."

"YOU ARE MY CHILD!" His words rumbled like thunder.

"You are MY child," He whispered.

"You are my CHILD," He tenderly finished.

She understood and responded with joy, "My Abba."

She woke under an immense, star-filled sky with tears of joy tracing clean paths down her face. In awe, she examined the sparkling canopy of heaven as she wiped the tears aside.

The clouds rolled away, disappearing into the far horizon. William had spoken truthfully. Christa had never seen such beauty as the stars from Ash Island. They were as countless as the sands of the sea.

A quickening in her spirit whispered they were a picture of His vastness — He was so utterly beyond her comprehension and yet she could embrace Him as a trustworthy father.

A constellation formed and twinkled above her. It encircled her head as a crown of blazing light. His glory burned away the silken strip binding her hair, cascaded through and across her skin, blinding her.

Even as darkness enveloped her sight, His glorious light cleansed her of every sin and smudge. Little flecks of ash fell away, lit on holy fire and consumed by mercy.

His pervading peace deepened further still, filling her from the inside out. It would always remain.

Thanksgiving filled her heart, overflowed her lips, ascended to the outstretched dome above her as she raised her hands in worship of her King — not of the heavens, not for the gift of this cleansing, but for Him. Her first love, her true love now restored to His rightful place.

A deep knowing filled her as well, assuaging all pain and grief.

"You never left me. Thank You," she whispered.

Nestling in the cloak's warmth, she fell soundly asleep.

My Anchor Holds

Christa Lea did what so many of us do. Dressed in flesh suits, we love the gifts over the Giver. We worship and serve "created things rather than the Creator—who is forever praised" (Romans 1:25b). We fall short of the glory of God and serve little gods. What little "g" gods contend for your heart?

What did Christa Lea do to escape the shame she felt when her idols were revealed? In 1 John 1:9, we read that if we confess our sins, God "is faithful and just and will forgive us our sins and purify us from all unrighteousness." Have you confessed your sins to God?

"This is the message we have heard from him and declare to you: God is light; in him there is no darkness at all."
1 John 1:5

In Psalm 112:4, we read, "light dawns for the upright" and in 1 John 1:5 and 7, "God is light; in him there is no darkness at all...But if we walk in the light, as he is in the light, we have fellowship with one another, and the blood of Jesus, his Son, purifies us from all sin."

What verb tense do you see in these verses? That shows us that repentance is not "one and done." It is a posture for life. How can you cultivate this posture?

Chapter 11

Hill of Rest

"I delight greatly in the Lord... For he has clothed me with garments of salvation ..."
Isaiah 61:10

They woke the next morning to the trill of birds in the trees. Hundreds, no thousands, had come home to roost.

Small finches of every description and color filled the forest and were busy at work — little darts and flashes of every prismatic hue flew from branch to ground and back again, collecting needful materials for their little perfect nests.

Christa Lea heard their chirps and feathers fluttering as they flew by, but her vision was gone. Even still, she didn't panic. The fresh memory of her Father's cleansing work in the night filled her with peace. William was delighted as he welcomed the finches home.

"So much has changed this morning," he said, pointing to the sky.

"Look, it's clear... all clear. Never has Ash Island transformed this quickly! And the birds. Look at all the birds!"

"My brother, I can't see, but it is good, very good," she smiled, grateful for the all-engulfing freedom.

He turned toward her. Her countenance had fully changed — long auburn hair fell about her shoulders and all traces of ash had vanished. The King's peace covered her even though her blue eyes were sightless.

He didn't have to ask. He knew the Crown of Beauty when he saw it. But this blindness was something new. It made him wonder, yet he trusted and didn't question.

They praised their Abba together.

"Hold on to this as I lead you, Christa Lea."

She nodded as he placed the end of a leather strap in her hand. He tied the other end around his waist. They passed through the forest and worked slowly up a gradual hill to an ancient well.

He hoisted the bucket up by its rope and, taking the ladle, filled it and served her first. She cupped it, drank, and returned it to him. They sat and shared the dipper, enjoying the beauty of the surrounding rebirth. He dug out bread, broke it, and giving thanks, they ate.

The sun shone upon the small clearing, illuminating the top of the small slope where they rested.

"This is a pleasant place. What is its name?" she asked.

He smiled, "Can you guess?"

"Is it the Well of Glory? I've heard rumors," she said.

"Yes, on the Hill of Rest. I have never drunk from it this soon. You have accepted the truth about yourself quickly. It is a gift to be teachable — to listen and learn, and when necessary to repent. And I am sure your response has immensely pleased Him!"

He broke into song:

"Your Spirit, oh, Lord God, is upon me.

You've anointed me to preach good news to the poor.

You gave her a crown of beauty for ashes and the oil of joy for mourning."

Christa rejoiced in the well-known hymn taken from the King's Book, marveling at its deep truth and beauty.

My song, she realized overwhelmed by His great love. She joined him.

"You clothe us in garments of praise... and we are Your planting.

We rejoice in You, oh, Lord!

You clothe us in garments of salvation - robed in Your righteousness!

You, Lord God, cause righteousness and praise to spring up before all the nations!"

When they finished worshiping, William took her water skin and filled it from the well, then gathered their things. She took hold of the leather strap and he led her once again.

They wound along the path for hours soaking in the sun's warmth. In this way, they slowly and carefully made their way to The Falls. He told her they must pass over them to get to his outpost.

My Anchor Holds

Christa Lea's peace is restored but her sight is not. In your experience, is it possible to have peace without seeing what is before you?

William tells Christa Lea that he had not ever gone so quickly from the place of shame to drink from the Well of Glory on the Hill of Rest. This was possible because she accepted the hard truth about herself. Have you ever faced hard truths about yourself and then found rest and refreshment "so soon"?

"This is what the Sovereign LORD, the Holy One of Israel, says: "In repentance and rest is your salvation, in quietness and trust is your strength."
Isaiah 30:15

In Isaiah 30:15, we read, "This is what the Sovereign LORD, the Holy One of Israel, says: "In repentance and rest is your salvation, in quietness and trust is your strength." When have you experienced this reality?

Chapter 12

The Falls

"For whoever does the will of my Father in heaven is my brother and sister and mother."
Matthew 12:50

As Christa Lea followed William he taught her about the island's wildlife — their names and habits. How some lived in hollow logs while others dug out places in the earth. He was very knowledgeable about Ash Island and its various inhabitants.

"How long have you been here?" she asked.

"Oh, nigh 14 years. You are my fifth guest," he answered with a smile in his voice.

"Has it been lonely work?"

He considered her, appraising her blank eyes and sincere question.

"No, it's just what I wanted."

Without speaking, they painstakingly made their way uphill. After several hours, they reached an open ridge top, a roar before them.

"We are at The Falls' pass," he shouted.

Before them lay a shimmering river which danced over stones before dropping 50 feet into the sea.

Below, sunlight sprinkled across the waterfall's surface refracting into rainbow prisms as the water sprayed upward. Waves crashed simultaneously, rolling and foaming below. Such a roar!

"The river comes from a spring-fed lake near my outpost. There's no way around it. We must cross it to get home but we'll stop here for tonight," William said, wiping the sweat from his forehead.

Christa Lea was also warm from the climb and wearily sat down. As she did, her cloak slipped aside, exposing her shoulder. William quickly covered it as she blushed.

He turned away confused at an awakening desire for her.

My sister, he chastised himself. *I'm sorry, my King.*

Having confessed it, he then regarded her perseverance and strength, admiring her ability to keep up, even though blind.

She is strong and beautiful, he admitted.

Tenderness for Christa stirred within him. He wanted to clamp the feeling tightly, as with a vise. It must not grow — to love another leads only to heartache.

A gentle breeze brushed his face, calming his spirit. He looked away and wiped tears from his eyes.

They set up camp for the night, built a fire, and prepared dinner.

Under the stars, the wood crackled and warmed them as the waves roared.

My Anchor Holds

Even faithful, resolved William must "take every thought captive unto obedience to Jesus Christ" (2 Corinthians 10:5). Is it more encouraging or discouraging to know that even the most seasoned saints must reign in their thoughts? Does it help to remember Christ's blessing for the pure in heart, that "they shall see God" (Matthew 5:8)?

In Solomon's Song of Songs (2:7, 3:5, 8:4) there is this repeated charge: "Do not arouse or awaken love until it so desires." What do you think that means?

"To love at all is to be vulnerable. Love anything and your heart will be wrung and possibly broken. If you want to make sure of keeping it intact you must give it to no one, not even an animal. Wrap it carefully round with hobbies and little luxuries; avoid all entanglements. Lock it up safe in the casket or coffin of your selfishness. But in that casket, safe, dark, motionless, airless, it will change. It will not be broken; it will become unbreakable, impenetrable, irredeemable. To love is to be vulnerable."

C. S. Lewis

How would you square the Song of Solomon refrain with this Lewis quote?

In what relationships have you paid this high price for love? Was your vulnerability "worth it"?

Chapter 13

CROSSING OVER

"Trust in him at all times, you people; pour out your hearts to him, for God is our refuge."
Psalm 62:8

"One last day of travel. Are you ready?" he asked Christa Lea the next morning.

William tied the thong of leather around his waist then secured it around hers.

He continued, "Just like the climb up here, I will direct you step by step, okay?"

She was struggling with her emotions — her peace had faltered in the night. Once again, she had relived the shipwreck as a nightmare tore her gifts away and left her suffocating in the ocean's depths. She cried for help and the King came immediately.

She woke to the roar of the falls. She thought the sound had infiltrated her dreams triggering the fearful phantasms. Although His peace remained, she felt apprehensive about what lay ahead.

"Ready?" he repeated.

She took hold of the leather lifeline between them with both hands, "Yes... okay."

She must trust William, for both their sakes.

He stepped into the river and turned back to her.

"It's not deep in some places, but is in others. At those places, be careful to do exactly as I say."

She nodded and moved into the water behind him. He placed her hand onto his right shoulder, muttered a prayer, and faced the pass.

Carefully, they advanced. A painful memory surfaced. He froze trying to dismiss it — a time when other lives had hung in the balance.

The grief wouldn't be denied and for a moment, which felt like an eternity, he relived the violent storm which had overtaken him at sea.

His precious cargo, his pregnant young wife. The violent waves lifted and tossed their small vessel. He had reached for her as a rolling wave rose above them.

Her fingers slipped through his. Lightning cracked overhead illuminating her fear-filled, desperate eyes. The next moment she was swept away, and with her, their unborn child.

Afterwards, grief-stricken and battle weary, he'd requested a place of solace to serve his King. His assignment: Ash Island.

He desired to rescue others because he failed the one person he loved most in the world. His Father understood and agreed.

The pressure of Christa Lea's hand on his shoulder brought him back to the present trial. Turning his face to her he yelled the next steps.

She nodded, lips set and jaw tight. One enormous step to the next rock. She would have to let go. There was room for both once they reached it, he assured.

They made it and repeated the same action two more times. Now they were in the middle of The Falls.

This would be the trickiest part. They would have to leap to make the next outcropping. She blanched while weakly nodding.

"Father, I am Yours," she whispered reverently. "I trust You."

He jumped first. The cord grew taut. She clutched it tightly.

After landing, he turned and yelled, "Jump now."

She turned toward his voice, steeled herself, and leapt.

In midair she heard her Father's clear command.

"Let go!"

She instantly let go of the line between them, joy flooding her as she trusted the direction. The outcome was never hers to engineer — she needed only to obey. The moment she threw her arms up, her sight returned.

She fell short. William instinctively leapt toward her, grasping her in both arms. The current swept them away. But he would not let go for anything. Not this time.

The water swiftly carried them toward the edge as the roar grew louder. At the last moment, the leather strap caught on a rock outcropping and held fast.

She clung to him as he pulled hand over hand, reeling them in toward the rock.

He grabbed the stone lip and helped her climb to safety and then pulled himself up. Their hearts raced. He held her close and looked into her seeing eyes.

"So be it," he whispered to his Father.

His own relinquishment brought freedom as well—he could love again without fear. He knew their mutual trust in God could lead to a marriage of fruitful service if that was their Father's will.

My Anchor Holds

Christa Lea's peace faltered, even after great days of strong faith. Ours does too. What steps do you take to strengthen your heart when emotions grow dark? ______________________________

"For we walk by faith not by sight" (2 Corinthians 5:7, ESV). Christa Lea walked by faith through the river. What does it look like today for you to walk by faith, not by sight?

"For we walk by faith not by sight."
2 Corinthians 5:7, ESV

When did Christa Lea's sight return? How is that symbolic of our faith walk?

Chapter 14

Home

"Listen, daughter, and pay careful attention: Forget your people and your father's house. Let the king be enthralled by your beauty; honor him, for he is your Lord."
Psalms 45:10-11

The rest of their journey passed without incident.

William's cottage sat beside a placid, green lake nestled within an extinct crater. Next door, its sister volcano steadily puffed smoke and occasionally rumbled.

Christa Lea was pleased to find fresh clothes waiting in a lovely room within the small stone outpost. And on the bed, a cozy quilt and feather down pillows. These were welcome comforts after camping on the hard ground.

The fire crackled as William stoked it. She sat curled in the blanket and admired its stitchery — he'd sewn a map of Ash Island into the top.

"There are unexpected and painful things in life we can't prepare for — shipwrecks... loss... when we relinquish our disappointment and grief, is He trustworthy to comfort and help?"

"Yes, He is," she knew firsthand.

He sat down opposite her in front of the cozy fireplace. Each night they'd gotten into the habit of reading His Word and discussing it.

"I didn't understand Abba's love for me. I thought it was tied to what I did for him," she continued. "We do works for Him, but they can't earn the salvation He has given as a gift."

He nodded in understanding.

"I find my home in doing His will, but He provided the home. I find such freedom and rest as I obey Him," he said.

As they continued the discussion, she ran her fingers over the island's outline. Its details were perfect and exquisite. The vibrant contrasts of black and green threads were vivid illustrations of loss and restoration.

"Perhaps," she ventured, "pain and grief are stark and necessary frames to contrast joy and peace so we may understand His mercy? And to appreciate what it cost Him..."

"Perhaps so," he agreed with a satisfied sigh.

The next day, a message came by carrier pigeon announcing the King's soon arrival. Each day they waited expectantly looking out toward the horizon.

A week later, William spotted the King's royal purple banners nobly waving on the masts of His fleet. William hadn't seen Him since being stationed here so long ago.

Deepened, he realized. *My love for Him has only deepened during this time.*

The couple made their way to the northern shore to welcome Him. The crystal beach glowed under the reflection of the sun.

As the King and His entourage rowed ashore, Christa Lea and William beamed with joy. His smile radiated happiness with and for them.

After He disembarked, they humbly knelt at His feet. He cupped their chins and raised their joyful faces to meet His.

"Well done," He spoke to each in turn.

Raising them to their feet, He embraced them.

"My daughter. My son."

Their hearts blazed with love as they hugged Him back.

"I have something for you."

William glanced at Christa Lea as the King took something from within a pocket in His royal robe. In His Hand lay two gold rings tied together with a purple satin ribbon, He placed them on William's open palm.

"It would give me great pleasure to unite you in marriage."

Christa Lea smiled at William, joy overflowing her heart. William considered the delicate bands and without hesitation answered for them both.

"Yes, please."

Their Abba performed the wedding ceremony, as gulls cried overhead, and the lapping of waves underscored their vows to Him and one another.

"Until death do us part."

William and Christa Lea gazed at the rings on one another's fingers — visual declarations of their spoken covenant. The courtiers and crews cheered.

A wedding feast was rowed ashore amid great joy.

"Would you like to come back with me?" The King asked.

"Your will is our will, Lord," William and Christa Lea answered in unison.

This was only the beginning of their adventures together with their Abba King.

My Anchor Holds

"I run in the path of your commandments, for you have set my heart free" (Psalm 119:32, New Heart Bible). How does this verse express our new relationship with "doing the good works God has prepared for us to do"?

Christa Lea considers that pain and grief may be "stark and necessary frames to contrast joy and peace so we may understand His mercy." Has this been your experience, that the grief you experienced helped you appreciate the depths of God's great mercy?

"I desire to do your will, my God; your law is within my heart." Psalm 40:8

"I desire to do your will, my God; your law is within my heart" (Psalm 40:8). This is the goal for every servant of the King. "Make your will my desire," is a prayer that we can pray that God will answer. Will you pray it now, as we conclude this tale?

Dear Reader,

Thank you for making this journey through Ash Island with us. We pray it has quickened your desire to know the only King who can redeem beauty from ashes, create joy from mourning, and trade your heaviness for His praise. To this King, the Lord Jesus, be all glory and honor forever.

Maybe you have turned this last page and realize you have not opened your heart to the King. Maybe you realize that you have not humbled yourself and received him as your Savior and Lord. Maybe today is your day to become His child.

If you have never trusted in Jesus Christ as your Lord and Savior, will you heed the Holy Spirit as He speaks to your heart? Jesus told a seeker named Nicodemus, "You must be born again" (John 3:7). In Romans 10:9, Paul explained, "If you declare with your mouth, 'Jesus is Lord,' and believe in your heart that God raised him from the dead, you will be saved." It is that simple.

Will you pray a prayer of repentance and faith and become a new creation in Christ today? It might sound something like this,

"Dear God, You are the only King. You have brought me to my own Ash Island. Now I see my need to be right with You on Your terms. I confess that I have sinned against You, fallen short of reflecting Your goodness and glory.

Sometimes I have proudly thought I could become Your child on the basis of what I do. This is not true. Only You can give me new life. Only You can forgive me and cleanse me.

Heavenly Father, I believe You sent Your beloved Son Jesus to die for my sins, as an acceptable substitute and sacrifice for me. I believe that You raised Him from the dead and I confess that Jesus is Lord. Thank You for saving my soul. Please Holy Spirit, help me walk in newness of life until I am with You face to face, in heaven forevermore. Amen."

"Yet to all who did receive him, to those who believed in his name, he gave the right to become children of God— children born not of natural descent, nor of human decision or a husband's will, but born of God."

—John 1:12-13

The End...

WITH GRATITUDE...

I am so grateful for my husband, Lane, our dear family, and treasured friends who have contributed to this book knowingly and unknowingly through their actions, prayers, and displays of love for our Lord and Savior, Jesus Christ.

And especially for Julie and Steven whose grateful hearts have experienced and continually hope for answered prayers as He creates "beauty from ashes."

Consider...

... special thanks to Debbie Smith, my dear editor-friend.

And to Abigail K. See who read and thoughtfully created the artwork for this small book.

And to Abigail Wallace who said, "Yes!"

And to Cassidy Wierks who brought her beautiful touch to the cover work for this edition.

And thank you especially to the reader. May our message bring encouragement and healing through His mighty working power for His glory, your good, and our joy.

Sarah L. Frantz, August 2024

Sarah L. Frantz is the debut and award-winning author of The Quickening, Overcomers Book 1.

She and her husband of 30 plus years live in the hills of Green Country, Oklahoma where she delights in serving others at Jesus' table through penned words, actions of love, and encouraging conversation.

Abigail Wallace is a Scripture-soaked writer, joy stalker and Bible teacher who stands, falls and gets back up in grace.

She is the thoughtful creator of Ash Island's reflection questions within "My Anchor Holds" and composed the "Dear Reader" and companion prayer.

Abigail loves to help others find hope in the Lord, as they take God at His word. She lives with her husband and two teen sons in rural Wisconsin.

You can find her book "MEEK NOT WEAK: A 12-Week Guide to the Gentle Strength of Meekness" at Amazon.

Abigail See was raised in rural Oklahoma and is a Jesus-loving, nature-drawing artist.

She enjoys painting His beauty in creation. This is her debut work.

You may learn more about her @shades_of_earth_art.

Made in the USA
Monee, IL
20 October 2024

383b092c-d783-4621-b3ca-de45f85d9146R01